LIKE A MACCABEE

ADVANCE PRAISE FOR LIKE A MACCABEE

Like a Maccabee is a refreshingly proud Jewish story. Barbara Bietz has given the miracles of Hanukkah new meaning for today's 'goal'-oriented children. She has bridged the generation gap in a warm true-sounding story of a boy, his grandfather and the special way they share a holiday. Highly recommended.

> Mindy Aber Barad
> author of *Jewish Humor Stories for Kids*
> Judaica Librarians' Choice Award Nominee

"Recommended! *Like a Maccabee* brings the spirit of Hanukkah into a contemporary story that every elementary student will relate to. Barbara Bietz creates memorable, likable characters that will be easy for parents and teachers—as well as their children—to recognize."

> Gabrielle Kaplan-Mayer
> author of *The Magic Tanach and Other Short Plays*

"Barbara Bietz has crafted a story that will resonate with all ages and make their hearts smile! Her multi-generational characters are refreshing and recognizable. Their voices make you laugh, pique your curiosity and feel compassion for others. Ben and Grandpa hit home runs when they develop the strength and courage to meet the challenges of change, a bully, and disappointment in their lives. This book is a 'love' gift for Hanukkah and for sharing a 'championship' life with those you love."

> Sheila N. Glazov
> author of *Princess Shayna's Invisible Visible Gift*

LIKE A MACCABEE

by Barbara Bietz

illustrations by Anita White

Yotzeret Publishing
St. Paul

LIKE A MACCABEE. Text copyright © 2006 by Barbara Bietz.
Interior illustrations copyright © 2006 by Anita White.
Cover illustration copyright © 2012 by Aleksey Vl B. Used under license from Shutterstock.com.

Editor: Leslie Martin
Book design: Sheyna Galyan
The tzaddi logo is a trademark of Yotzeret Publishing, Inc.

Library of Congress Control Number: 2006904740
Publisher's Cataloging-in-Publication Data:
Bietz, Barbara.
   Like a Maccabee / by Barbara Bietz ; illustrations by Anita White.
   p. cm.
   ISBN 1-59287-136-4
   ISBN 13 978-1-59287-136-0
   Summary: Days before Hanukkah, ten-year-old Ben prepares for his championship soccer game while pursued by the school bully and adjusting to a new roommate: his grandfather.
[1. Family life--Fiction. 2. Hanukkah--Fiction 3. Jews--Fiction. 4. Soccer--Fiction. 5. Bullying--Fiction.] I. White, Anita I. II. Title.
PZ7.B47752 Li 2006
813.54-dc22   2006904740

For Jillian and Trevor for being my sources of
inspiration, Jonathan for his encouragement,
and for Kenny, Connie and Sylvia, the
grandparents who are a blessing to us all.
A special thanks to my writing friends
for their ongoing support.
—B.B.

CONTENTS

One
LATE AGAIN

I should have said yes when Nick offered me a ride home. By the time I saw Mom's blue van, the field was dark and street lights dotted the parking lot. Shivering, I zipped up my jacket and packed my soccer gear.

Coach waved when he saw Mom pull up.

I was the last kid to leave. I jogged to the van and threw my soccer bag on the floor.

"Sorry we're late, Ben," Mom said as she turned down the radio. "We had some Hanukkah shopping to do and Grandpa was tired so I took him home before coming for you."

I just shrugged. What was I supposed to say? I wanted to say that I was sick and tired of waiting in the freezing cold while my coach kept checking his watch. "Late" had become a way of life since Grandpa came to stay. Grandpa is my dad's dad. Mom and Dad had been asking Grandpa to move in with us since Grandma died two years ago, and now he was here for good. I thought it would be great when Mom quit her job at the bank so she could be home. Boy, was I wrong about that!

"Daddy's making latkes tonight! He's practicing for Hanukkah!" my sister Mandy shouted.

"That's great, Munchkin," I said, clicking the seat belt around my waist. When I was Mandy's age I got excited about Hanukkah, too. I still liked the potato latkes, and all of the presents, of course. But I turned ten on my last birthday, and that's a little too old to get wound up about silly kid songs and plastic dreidel decorations. Besides, we only get our big presents at the end of the holiday. The first few days we get stupid stuff like pencils or toothbrushes.

"So, how was practice?" Mom asked.

"Okay. Coach told us we made the finals for league championship." I stared out the van window.

Mom stopped the van at a red light. "That's terrific news. Why don't you sound more excited?"

I shook my head. "We don't stand a chance. We're playing the Bulldogs. One of their defenders is this huge kid named Travis. Everyone calls him Travis the Tank. He's fierce and he's fearless. We're going to get killed."

"Just do your best, Ben. I'm sure it will be fine. The Eagles have had a great season," Mom said.

She didn't get it. I worked hard all season to become a starter. We made it to the finals, and now I was about to be destroyed by Tank.

Mom said, "We have a lot to do this week," as if she hadn't heard a thing I said about soccer.

"Soccer is silly," Mandy said as she patted the pink tutu she was wearing over her jeans. "Ballet is better."

"Yeah, no kidding. We all know you like ballet. You wear that tutu twenty-four seven."

Mandy scrunched up her face. "Mommy, Ben is being mean."

"I'm not being mean," I said. "You do wear that thing all the time."

Mandy crossed her arms over her chest.

Mom said, "Kids, please. It's been a long day. Let's just enjoy a quiet ride home."

I really didn't want to fight with a five-year-old, or Mom for that matter. The van suddenly felt stuffy. I opened the window a little to let in a sliver of cold air so I could breathe again.

For the rest of the ride home Mandy sang "I Have a Little Dreidel" at least ten times, each verse louder than the one before.

When Mom finally pulled into our driveway, I couldn't wait to bolt out of the van.

Two
ROOM FOR GRANDPA

The house smelled of potatoes and sweet onions. Dad's latkes sizzled in hot oil, splattering in the frying pan like Fourth of July sparklers.

I dumped my soccer gear on the kitchen floor.

"New apron, Dad?"

It was bright blue fabric with pictures of dancing menorahs on it, and a big dreidel shaped pocket in front.

"Yup. And don't roll your eyes, Ben. I think it's very festive! I bought it at the community center holiday boutique." Dad beamed like a little kid with a new toy. He works as a director at the neighborhood community center, and he feels like he has to buy stuff at every holiday boutique. Year after year he brings home something more bizarre than the year before.

"I like your apron, Daddy," Mandy said. "It makes you look like a happy cook." She made a face at me.

"Thank you, Princess. You have excellent taste," Dad said. He flipped a sizzling latke.

"Dad, aren't we starting with all the Hanukkah stuff a little early?" I sat down and kicked off my cleats.

Dad grinned. "I'm trying a new latke recipe. I don't want to take any chances!" he said.

"Kids, go wash up." Mom said. "And Ben, put away your soccer things, and please stop taking off those muddy shoes in the house. Oh, and call Grandpa down, too. He's resting in his room."

7

His room? Grandpa had only been at our house for a few weeks and already it was "his room." No one even asked me if I minded sharing my room with Grandpa. They just told me he was moving in.

The bedroom door was closed. It felt weird to knock on my own door, like I was an intruder. It didn't matter that behind the door were my things, my bed, my books and my trophies. When Grandpa lived in Chicago he would visit a few times a year. He moved in with us because the winters in Chicago weren't good for his health. Now Grandpa was in our house all the time, like a piece of furniture plunked down in the middle of a room that you keep stubbing your toe on because you can't get used to it being there.

I knocked lightly on the door. "Grandpa, are you awake?"

"Yes. Hello, my boychik. Come in," Grandpa said as he opened the door. The smell of his aftershave bit my nose. He looked funny without his glasses, sort of like a turtle without its shell. His hair was messy and his clothes were all rumpled.

I forced a smile. "Boychik" is the Yiddish name that Grandpa had called me since I was little. Hearing it now was really annoying, like Grandpa thought I was still six years old. He might be my grandpa but he felt more like a stranger. Maybe not a complete stranger, but it was almost as weird as if the crossing guard from school had moved in. I've seen that guy every day since kindergarten, but I wouldn't want to share my room with him.

"Mom said to call you down for dinner." I threw my soccer stuff next to my bed.

"Thank you for coming to get me. I was just having a little snooze." Grandpa let out a little sigh and rubbed his eyes.

"How was your day?" Grandpa asked. He patted me on the head like a puppy.

"It was okay." I nodded, partly so I could get my head out from under Grandpa's hand. "My soccer team is in the finals." I was pretty sure Grandpa couldn't care less about soccer.

"Well, mazel tov! This is very exciting. You Eagles must be a fine team," Grandpa said, pointing to my practice jersey.

I had to give Grandpa credit for at least trying to sound interested. "I don't know." I shrugged. "I think we're gonna get creamed."

"Why?" he asked.

"The other team has the best defender in the whole league."

"Oh, I see," Grandpa said, as he put on his glasses. "So does that mean you can't win?"

I shook my head. "Grandpa, I'm a center forward. My job is to score goals. Travis the Tank is a defender. His job is to squash anyone that gets in his way. Everyone's afraid of him. I don't think we have a chance."

"Hmm." Grandpa said, as he plumped up the pillow on his bed. "I know of someone who was in a similar situation."

"Really?" I wondered who Grandpa knew that played soccer.

"Yes, someone who lived a very long time ago."

"Who?"

"Judah Maccabee," Grandpa said.

Judah Maccabee? Either Grandpa really didn't understand a thing about soccer, or he was getting so old he forgot what we were talking about. I didn't remember everything about the Hanukkah story, but I was pretty sure Judah Maccabee didn't play soccer.

Then Grandpa said, "Judah Maccabee had to work very hard to accomplish his goals, too."

I felt a boring speech coming on. "Let's go have dinner," I said. "We can talk about soccer later."

I hoped Grandpa didn't realize I was avoiding his lecture.

Three
MY *ROOM*

We said a short prayer in Hebrew before dinner. We never used to do that before Grandpa came. I didn't mind. It just seemed a little goofy to me. It's not like we talked about it, or made a decision like, "Hey, let's start saying a prayer before we eat." We just started doing it. We also light candles every Friday night for Shabbat. Before Grandpa came we would only do it if we had company.

Dad's potato latkes were crispy brown and delicious, as good as having dessert for dinner. I ate mine with a mountain of sour cream.

"Well," Mom said as she spooned applesauce onto Mandy's plate, "we have a lot to do. It's hard to believe Hanukkah starts this week!"

"Yay! I love Hanukkah!" Mandy cried, clapping her hands wildly. She managed to knock a fork onto her lap, splattering sour cream on her tutu.

"Oh no!" she said and put her arms in the air.

Mom stuck her napkin in her water glass and wiped off Mandy's tutu. Still patting Mandy's spill, Mom looked at me. "Tomorrow I think we'll go to the mall after school. I'd like to get some things and it would be a nice outing for Grandpa. You don't have soccer, do you?"

"Tomorrow's good," I said, nodding my head. At least she didn't ask me to miss a practice. "Can Nick come?"

"Sure, you can ask Nick," Mom said.

"Hey, Ben," Dad said. "Mom told me about your big game. I'm so proud of you! Good job!"

"Thanks, Dad, I guess it is good news."

Dad patted the corners of his mouth with a napkin that was tucked into the top of his shirt. "I heard there's a huge kid on the other team."

"Yeah, his name is Travis."

"Oh yeah, Travis the Crank. That's the one Mom mentioned."

"Not exactly. It's Travis the Tank. He's a defender for the Bulldogs. He goes to my school. He's enormous and he steals the ball from everyone."

"That's so mean," Mandy piped up. "The kids in my class get a time-out for stealing. You should tell Crank's teacher. He's gonna get in trouble for stealing the ball." She shook her index finger in the air like a bossy kindergarten teacher.

I put my face in my hands and closed my eyes. Could there possibly be a family any-

where that understood less about soccer than mine did?

When I looked up I saw Mom pouring Grandpa a cup of tea. As Grandpa lifted the cup to his mouth, his eyes met mine. He winked at me. I wasn't sure why.

While Mom and Dad cleaned up, Grandpa read the newspaper at the table and sipped his tea. When Mandy started spinning around like a dizzy ballerina, I went upstairs to do my homework. I could only take so much family togetherness.

I had almost finished my social studies chapter about the Boston Tea Party when there was a knock on my door.

"Yeah?" I said.

Dad walked into my room and closed the door. "I think Grandpa's getting tired. Are you almost done studying?" He said it in a quiet voice.

I slammed my book shut. "Fine!" I threw my hands up in the air. "I'm done."

Dad leaned in toward me. "This is hard for all of us."

"I know." Maybe he was right. It was hard, but mostly for me. I grabbed my social studies book and went downstairs to finish reading. When I was done, I went upstairs to the bathroom to get ready for bed. Mandy was brushing her teeth with her pink ballerina electric toothbrush. I quickly washed my face and brushed my teeth.

"You aah sho lucky," she said above the buzzing. Toothpaste dripped from her lower lip.

I was almost afraid to ask. "Why?"

She turned her toothbrush off and spit light green goop into the sink.

"Because you get to share with Grandpa. I wish I had two beds in my room."

I just looked at her. "Good night, Munchkin." I quickly left the bathroom.

Walking past Mom and Dad's room, I could hear their voices. I knocked on the door. Then it got really quiet. They didn't even open the door.

"Goodnight," I called out.

They said goodnight through the door.

Grandpa was already asleep when I got back to my room. I could hear his breathing. Every breath he took sounded like a snort going in and a whistle coming out. I tried really hard not to let it annoy me.

Four
TANK STRIKES

The next day at lunch, Nick and I walked through the line together with our trays resting on the metal bars. "I wish we were playing a different team next week," I said. "Any team but the Bulldogs." I picked up an apple from the giant fruit bowl while the cafeteria lady put spaghetti on Nick's plate.

"C'mon, Ben. We can beat them. Tank may be big, but you're the one with brains. Coach always says you know how to use your head." Nick tapped my head with his finger.

"Yeah. Tell Mr. Matthews that. I just got a C on my social studies test." Actually, it was a C-, but I couldn't bring myself to admit that out loud.

We picked up our trays and headed for the tables.

The lunchroom was crowded. We could only find seats near the door. Every time someone came into the lunchroom, we got a blast of cold air.

"We need to go through the line faster to get a better spot," I said.

Nick wasn't listening. "Hey, look."

I glanced up from my lunch to see Tank strutting through the cafeteria. Two smaller kids walked with him like little soldiers under his command.

"Is he coming over to us?" Nick's voice shook a little.

"I sure hope not," I mumbled.

A few seconds later, Tank was staring down at me, like a dog that just found a lamb chop in the garbage.

"Hey, Len," he said.

"My name is Ben."

Nick kicked my foot under the table as if to say "Let him call you Len."

"Whatever. Len, Ben. Close enough. I hear you guys are playing us. You're the center forward, right?" Tank barked.

I nodded. "Yup."

"Well, good luck."

I wrinkled my forehead. Could it be that Tank was actually a good sport?

"Yeah, you too," I said with a little smile.

"You're the only one who needs it, loser," said Tank. Then he leaned in, so close that I could see a scar on his eyebrow. "You'll never get the ball past me." Tank snickered as he took the apple off my tray and threw it to one of his sidekicks like a baseball. They laughed and pointed as they walked off tossing my apple back and forth.

I wanted to say something, to shout at them, but no words came out. I just watched it all happen.

"Hey, look at Len," Tank called out to his friends. He held his hands over his mouth like a megaphone. "He can't even get his apple back. He'll be pitiful with a soccer ball."

I didn't budge. I just sat like a rock and stared as though Tank had not only swiped my fruit, but had also tied my feet to the bench. A volcano erupted in my stomach.

"What a jerk," Nick said.

"Yeah." I let out a deep breath, like a deflating balloon. "A jerk that's about to win a soccer game."

Five
ONE MORE THING

Lunch was finally over, but I felt like my troubles had just begun. Not only was I worried about losing the game, but Tank had made me look like an idiot and would never let me forget it.

Back in the classroom, it took a few minutes for everyone to settle down. Our classroom always smelled funny after lunch, like someone put a leftover lunch bag in the closet with tuna or spoiled fruit, or something else stinky still left inside. Mr. Matthews never seemed to notice, like his nose didn't work.

The other weird thing about Mr. Matthews was that he used his fist to erase the marker from the board, instead of a real eraser or even a rag. His hand was always streaked with black.

We sat at desks with spaces for our books and supplies underneath. Nick sat two rows away from me. I watched him try to pass a note to Jason, a midfielder on our team. "Hey Jason, catch," he whispered.

Jason opened the note and started cracking up. He wrote something on the paper, and whispered back, "Nick, heads up."

Nick read the note, then stuck it in his desk. He gave Jason the thumbs up sign. How could they goof around when our future was doomed?

Mr. Matthews was talking about something, but I wasn't listening. I had important stuff to think about and long division wasn't part of it. For a while, I counted the little holes in the ceiling tiles, and then I stared at the words

"Our History, Our World" on the social studies board.

I thought I heard my name. I looked up at Mr. Matthews.

"Well?" he said. He lifted his fuzzy eyebrows. "Ben, do you have an answer?"

"Um, I um, can you repeat the question?" I was sunk.

Mr. Matthews shook his head. "Look at the problem on the board. What is the next step?" He pointed to the equation with his long stick.

I looked at the problem but my mind went blank. It's not that I didn't know how to do it, I just couldn't think. I bit my lip. Everyone stared at me, including Mr. Matthews.

But then he said, "That's okay, Ben, this is a tricky one. I'll come back to you." His face softened a little.

Thank you, Mr. Matthews, for giving me a break. I turned to look at Nick. Blair, the girl who sits behind Nick, smiled at me. I quickly turned away. I was afraid she would start laughing at me over the math problem fiasco, but she didn't.

Then Mr. Matthews said, "I have an announcement to make and I would like everyone's attention."

I decided to listen. I didn't need any more aggravation.

"As we all know, this is the holiday season." He pointed to the bulletin boards on the far wall. One was decorated with candy canes and greenery, one with a menorah. Another had paintings of Kwanzaa candles. "All families have different traditions they celebrate. We are starting something new this year called the Family Celebration Project. Each of you will be responsible for an oral presentation describing a family tradition. It can be about a traditional holiday or not. It can be a ceremony, a special meal, or just something unique that your family does together. Along with the oral presentation, you must create a visual aid, such as a poster, collage or diorama."

Jason raised his hand but didn't wait for Mr. Matthews to call on him. He just blurted out, "What's a diorama? It sounds like something that would give me a really bad stomachache!"

Everyone started laughing and even Mr. Matthews smiled. "For those of you who are not familiar with a diorama, it is a model or presentation of a scene that you create inside a container, like a shoebox."

Mr. Matthews walked up and down the aisles handing out assignment sheets as he talked. He stopped at my desk and handed me a paper. "This is an opportunity to improve your social studies grade, which many of you could use." He looked right at me when he said it. "Your grade will be based on both the project and the presentation."

The class buzzed with voices. This was one of those assignments that some kids get really excited about.

"I know," Sammy said. "Maybe I'll make Christmas cookies to share. I help my Mom make them every year."

"My dad always takes pictures of us on our birthday," Blair said. "He marks our height on the wall in the kitchen. I think I'll measure everyone in the class." She pulled out a ruler from her desk and waved it around.

Jenny raised her hand to ask Mr. Matthews a question. When he called on her she said, "My family doesn't celebrate Kwanzaa, but I really want to. Does that count?" she asked.

Mr. Matthews shrugged. "I suppose if you help your family create a new tradition, that would be fine." He smiled like he was happy that the kids were so enthusiastic.

I wondered what in the world I would do. I mean, we celebrate Hanukkah, but what would I say? We light candles, eat latkes, open presents, THE END? Maybe this year I would get new underwear on the first night of Hanukkah. That's an inspiring tradition.

Or maybe I could tell the truth and say, "My family has a new custom of moving people into your room without permission. This is a unique tradition because it turns your world upside down and nobody cares."

Mr. Matthews put his hand up. "One more thing," he said. "We will have our presentations right after the Holiday Show, so parents are invited to attend."

My stomach dropped to my feet like an out-of-control elevator.

Six
The Mall

Mom picked me up from school to go to the mall. Nick couldn't come because he had band practice. He plays the saxophone, which is a pretty cool instrument, even though it's almost as big as he is. Nick tried to get me to join the school band once, but learning to read music seemed like extra homework to me.

Grandpa was in the front seat. I sat in the back with Mandy.

"How was school today?" Mom asked as I climbed into the van.

"Okay."

"Just okay?"

"Yup, just okay." I didn't feel like talking and no way did I want to say anything about Tank or the Family Celebration Project.

"I had a good day!" Mandy shouted.

"Great. I'm happy for you," I said, as if you can have a bad day in kindergarten.

"We did our ABCs, sang the worm song, and mixed paint colors." Mandy looked at me like I had asked for this information. "Then I came home and had lunch with Grandpa. He cut my sandwich into triangles, not squares like Mommy does. Isn't that funny?"

Grandpa turned around and smiled at Mandy. "Triangles taste better," he said.

Mandy giggled.

Was there something I wasn't getting here?

When we got to the mall, I jumped out of the van, ready to race to the food court for a snack. But I had to wait for everyone to get out of the van. Grandpa took forever, taking slow steps, one foot at a time. Slow motion shopping with Grandpa wasn't my idea of a good time.

The parking lot was decorated with green wreaths and shiny red bows on every pole. The department store Christmas tree stood tall in the window. A cardboard elf held a sign with the times when Santa Claus would be visiting the mall. Smaller windows were painted with reindeer and fake snow.

In the corner of one window was a little painted menorah with Happy Holidays written in silver letters.

I don't mind all the fuss about Christmas. But that painted menorah looked so sad, as if someone said, "Hey, we forgot to put up something for Hanukkah. Anyone know how to paint a menorah?" Like they did it at the last minute.

It seemed like an hour until we finally got to the mall entrance. For a weekday, it was pretty crowded. Stores had signs that said stuff like "Holiday Sale, Buy One Sweater, Get One Free," and "Don't Forget That Special Someone This Year." The escalator was full of shoppers. From far away, they looked like colorful caterpillars crawling up and down.

Mom said, "Let's go to the food court. Grandpa and I will save a table while you and Mandy get a snack."

When we got there, Mom picked a table right in the middle and wiped some crumbs off with a napkin. She handed me some money and said, "We can watch you from here, but please hold your sister's hand."

"Mom, no… that is so lame."

Mom gave me a look as she and Grandpa sat down. She meant business.

"Fine." I turned to Mandy and grabbed her hand. "Let's go."

Mandy squeezed my hand. "This is fun. What kind of snack do you want? I think I want ice cream, or maybe French fries, or a donut…"

"Slow down!" I said.

That kid could win a prize for speed talking.

"How about we each get a smoothie, and then share a big cookie?" I asked.

"Okay." She nodded her head and her ponytail bobbed up and down.

I walked Mandy to the Juicy-Juicy smoothie bar. The counter was decorated with multi-colored lights shaped like pieces of fruit.

"Munchkin, do you want yours in a kiddie cup with the dancing berries on it?" I asked.

Mandy jumped up and down. "Oh, yes, yes, yes, I do!"

I ordered two strawberry smoothies — one in a kiddie cup — and one giant chocolate chip cookie.

Mandy grinned from ear to ear. It was actually pretty fun being on our own, even though Mom could see us from where she sat.

After we walked to the other end of the counter to wait for our food I heard "Hey, Len. Is that your girlfriend? A little young, isn't she?"

The words pierced through my head. I turned around and Tank was in my face. I really thought I was going to throw up, right there in the food court. Our eyes met.

"You're nothing, dude," he said. His nostrils were flaring like a crazy dog.

I quickly looked toward Mom and Grandpa's table. They faced us, but I was saved by one of those giant potted plants that blocked their view of Tank.

Mandy pulled on my arm. She didn't even seem to notice that Tank was there. "Do you think we'll have time to shop for Hanukkah presents?"

Tank looked at me like I was dirt on his shoe. "Hanukkah shopping? Isn't that cute."

I wanted to punch him. If Mandy hadn't been with me, I might have been brave enough to do it. So what did I do instead? I stood there.

Tank gave my shoulder a little push.

I was about to push him back. I really was going to push him, but I saw Grandpa walking toward us.

"Boychik," Grandpa called, "would you mind ordering me an iced tea?"

Could this get any more embarrassing? I nodded at Grandpa. He turned to go back to his table.

"You're at the mall with your Gramps? Pathetic." Tank looked at me sideways and walked off.

I finally had a chance to stand up to Tank, and what happened? My slow-motion grandpa ruined it.

Mandy pulled on my arm again. "Who was that boy?" she asked.

"No one, just forget it. C'mon let's go order Grandpa's drink."

"He seems like a meanie. I do not like him, not one little bit." She shook her head back and forth.

Even though I was furious, with Tank and with myself, I smiled a little. "You're right, Munchkin. He is a meanie."

When we finally sat down I still felt a little shaky. I prayed that Mandy wouldn't say anything about Tank, and Grandpa wouldn't ask. I ate my snack in silence. I didn't feel like talking.

Mandy swung her legs, as she sipped her drink. "This is so yummy!" she shouted.

Mom was going over a list of things she needed to buy, and Grandpa kept moving his straw up and down in his iced tea. Every time the straw went through the plastic top it made a squeaking sound that made me cringe.

Finally Mom said, "I think we should get going. My list is longer than I thought." She started cleaning up the table and put our trash on the orange tray.

"Sounds good to me," said Grandpa. He took the tray and emptied it into the trash.

We did some shopping but I wasn't really paying attention. I kept turning around to see if Tank was behind me.

The whole way home I was trying to figure out if I was upset that Tank had bullied me again, or if I was just ticked off at myself for being so useless. Tank was really getting under my skin. I knew he was a creep, but he seemed to have this power over me. He was all I could think about.

Seven
NO 'I' IN TEAM

The next day I almost faked a sore throat so I wouldn't have to go to school, but then Mom wouldn't have let me go to practice. I told Nick I needed homework help and stayed in the classroom during morning recess and then again at lunch.

He bought my excuse at recess, but by lunch he was a little suspicious.

"Okay," he shrugged. "I'll eat with Jason."

I felt crummy as I watched him walk away, but it was better than facing Tank.

At practice, I was still mad about what had happened at the mall. When Coach split up the team for a scrimmage, I saw Tank everywhere. Every kid had his face. When I got the ball I ran like an angry bull.

Nick called out, "I'm open!"

Jason shouted, "Pass the ball!"

But I pushed on. I weaved my way past the other players toward the goal. I could do it alone. I'd show everyone I could be as tough as Tank. I took a shot. The ball sailed right over the goal. Furious, I kicked the grass as hard as I could. My toe hit the end of my cleat and it hurt.

I wouldn't let that missed goal stop me. I kept working hard. Jason got the ball and passed it to Nick. I called for the ball. It was like they didn't even hear me. Nick passed the ball to Eddie, which really annoyed me since I was wide open. Finally Eddie passed the ball to me, and I wouldn't let it go. I fought through three players and kept the ball. I kept dribbling toward the goal. I could hear the ball connecting with my foot. Bam! The ball flew right past the goalie. It was a clean shot in the middle of the net.

"Yes!" I shouted, holding my fists in the air. I felt victorious and I had done it on my own.

Coach blew his whistle.

Practice was over and the team packed up to leave.

Nick and Jason were playing dodge ball, laughing and goofing around while they waited for their rides home.

I saw Nick's mom pull up, and Jason's mom a few minutes later.

"See you, Ben," Nick shouted.

Jason waved at me.

I didn't say goodbye to anyone. I didn't want to. I practiced shooting goals until my cleats were caked with mud.

After everyone was gone, I was still waiting for my mom. Coach called me over.

"Hey, Ben?"

"Yeah, Coach?" I jogged to the sidelines.

"You were pretty intense during practice."

"Yeah." At least Coach knew how committed I was to doing my best.

"Well, with your attitude we have no chance of winning the game."

"What do you mean? I worked so hard!"

Did he even watch me during practice? I felt like he had hit me in the head with a soccer ball.

"That's your problem Ben," Coach said. "You said 'I worked so hard.' Well, there is no 'I' in team. Think about it." He walked off to the other side of the field.

The air turned ice cold. I put on my jacket. Where was Mom? If she had been on time for a change, Coach might never have given me that lecture. Finally, Mom's van pulled up. I jumped in.

"Sorry I'm late again, Ben. I had to take Grandpa to the doctor. It's been a long day."

I didn't say anything back but Mom didn't seem to notice. She just talked on about her busy day. I looked out the window, my jaw tightening. The thing about being mad is that it's really hard to stop the feeling. I felt like a hamster on a wheel, running hard and getting nowhere.

Eight
IN MY ROOM

At dinner, I stared at my plate and moved carrots around in circles with my fork. I could feel everyone staring at me, like I had that big "L" for "Loser" plastered on my forehead.

"Ben, do you want to help us with Hanukkah decorations? Daddy bought some new stuff," Mandy said.

"No, thanks," I said and let out a deep sigh.

"Are you okay?" Mom asked. "You're not eating."

I shrugged.

"How was soccer today?" she asked. I didn't answer.

"Ben, I know you're worried," she said, "but can't you be happy that your team made it this far? I ran into Mrs. Alden today and she said Nick is excited about being in the finals."

I slumped in my chair like a giant beanbag, and mumbled, "Yeah, well I'm not Nick."

She had no idea how I felt. I hate it when Mom tries to make me be like someone else, like I'm Mr. Potato Head, and all she has to do is stick a new hat on me, or give me a new pair of ears, or a big red smile, and I'd be the way she wants me to be.

"Hey, sport. Take it easy. It's just a game; it's supposed to be fun," Dad said. He patted me on the arm. Great advice from a guy who thinks a local chili cook-off is a sporting event.

I suppose if my coach didn't understand, I couldn't expect anything more from my clueless family.

"Oh, Ben," said Mom. "We got a notice today about the holiday festivities at your school. Sounds like fun." She put more carrots on my plate, even though I hadn't eaten the first helping. I wish she hadn't reminded me about that stupid Family Celebration Project.

"You don't have to come," I said. "It's not a big deal."

"Of course we'll come, sweetie. Maybe I'll even take Mandy out of her class so she can come, too. I think she'd enjoy it."

Great. I could just see it. My whole family standing in the back of the classroom while I made a complete fool of myself.

Dad said, "We have a wonderful modern art exhibit coming up at the community center." He cut a piece of his chicken.

I was relieved to have the focus off of me.

Dad turned to Grandpa. "Maybe you would like to join me? We're expecting quite a turnout, with artists from all over the city. Don't you think you would enjoy that?" Dad nodded his head up and down, like he was telling Grandpa he would enjoy it, not asking if he would.

"No thanks," said Grandpa. "That's really not my cup of tea." He sort of half-smiled like he was embarrassed to say no to Dad.

"It would be nice if we could find some interesting things for you to do," Dad said.

"Don't worry about me. I don't need a lot to be entertained." Grandpa wasn't smiling at all.

"Daddy," Mandy interrupted, "Grandpa doesn't have time to play with you. He's teaching me to play checkers and after that, Go Fish."

Grandpa patted Mandy's hand. "Yes, sweetheart. You keep your grandpa very busy."

"And I'm going to win when we play checkers!" Mandy said.

"Winning isn't everything, Mandy," Grandpa said. He looked at me.

Mom got up and brought a plate of Dad's cookies to the table.

I didn't want dessert; I already had a pain in my stomach. "I've got homework to do. Can I be excused?"

"Go ahead, Ben," Mom said.

As I got up Grandpa said, "Can I please be excused, too?"

Mandy burst out, "Grandpa, you're too old to ask permission to leave the table!"

Mom and Dad laughed. If things had been different, I might have laughed too.

Even though I had to figure out what to do for the Family Celebration Project, plus finish a ton of math homework, I couldn't wait to be alone.

Before I sat down at my desk, I looked around my room. Years of soccer pictures and trophies surrounded me. I walked over to the shelf and moved my trophies around so there was an open spot right in the middle. I wiped some dust off with my hand. A championship trophy would look so awesome there. Maybe I could leave the space open for good luck. Nah. I put the trophies back in their old spots.

There was a knock at the door. I flew back to my chair and opened my notebook so I would look busy. "Come in," I called.

"Hello, boychik." Grandpa stood at the door like he wasn't allowed in the room without asking first.

"Hey, Grandpa."

I didn't invite him in. Maybe if he stopped calling me boychik, I wouldn't feel so cranky. I just wanted to be alone.

As though he had read my mind, Grandpa said, "Mandy and your mother are downstairs hanging paper dreidels and cleaning the menorah." He held up a little blue tissue paper dreidel on a string, and then put it next to my notebook. "I think I'll join them." He smiled and closed the door.

I picked up the little dreidel and wound and unwound the string around my finger, then stuck it in my sweatshirt pocket. I wondered if Grandpa felt stuck hanging out with Mom and Mandy since I was in my room. Maybe he wanted to rest on his bed or something. Well, it was my room, after all.

The math problems stared at me, but my mind was buzzing with other things. My soccer coach was mad at me, Tank bullied me at school, and my family didn't understand a thing about me. Plus, I had this stupid project hanging over my head.

I forced myself to look up the answers to my homework in the back of the book and then quickly finished all the problems. I put my notebook and book in my backpack and threw it toward my bed. The backpack missed its destination and fell on the floor with a thud. I leaned over between my bed and Grandpa's to pick it up when I spotted something.

Underneath Grandpa's bed, pushed up against the wall, was a box the size of a small suitcase. What could it be? I looked over my shoulder to make sure that the bedroom door was closed. Then I put my desk chair against the door.

I knelt down on the floor and reached under the bed, trying not to disturb Grandpa's brown and orange crocheted blanket. I pulled out the brown cardboard box. It was taped closed and had a label that read "Personal."

I picked up the box and shook it a little. It wasn't very heavy, and it sounded like there were lots of papers and a few jingling things. What could be in there? Maybe I could take just a little peek. I pulled on the end of tape to see how easily it would open. The tape wouldn't stick back to the box.

I didn't want to pull it any further or Grandpa might figure out I had tried to look at his stuff. I peeked into the little opening. It was too small and too dark to see anything but it smelled old, like the stuff we find under the seats in Mom's van when we're looking for a lost library book.

I could hear voices from downstairs. I slid the box back to its spot, tossed my backpack on my bed and went to see what all the noise was about.

Nine
GRANDPA'S STORY

A string of multi-colored paper dreidels crowned the fireplace. The brightly polished silver menorah sat on the dining room table. Mandy skipped around tossing foil-covered chocolate coins all over the table while Dad stood on a ladder to hang "Happy Hanukkah" signs on the wall.

"Ben, did you see?" Mandy called out. "Daddy put all the presents out! Tomorrow night is Hanukkah. I can't wait one more minute!" She clapped her hands.

"Great," I answered and looked at the boxes wrapped in blue and white paper with a silver Star of David gift tag hanging from each one. I picked up the largest package and shook it. "Hey Munchkin, I think this big one is for you," I teased.

"Put it down!" she shouted. "You'll break it!"

"Okay, okay." I put the box back on the pile and took a seat in the chair across from Grandpa.

Mandy and Dad finished decorating and sat down, too. Mom brought in cocoa. I put my hands around the warm cup and took a sip. I admit it was kind of a relief to be out of my room.

"Grandpa, what did you do for Hanukkah when you were a little boy? Did you get presents?" Mandy asked.

"Not really. Sometimes my father would give us coins. My mama made potato latkes, of course. Mostly I would love to watch the candles burning while we sang songs, and my father would tell us all about Judah Maccabee and his brave army." Grandpa turned to me. "Do you kids know the story of Hanukkah?"

He said "kids" but I knew I was the one Grandpa expected to answer. I felt like faking a headache.

"Yeah, sure I do," I said. "The whole thing about the oil lasting eight days and all. It was a miracle or something."

"Ah," Grandpa said holding up his finger, "the story of the oil is only one miracle, only a part of the whole story of Hanukkah."

Grandpa sat up straight and his eyes lit up like candles as he spoke. It was hard to believe an old holiday tale would get him so excited. I didn't want to hurt his feelings, but listening to a boring story was the last thing I felt like doing. I looked at my watch. "Grandpa, maybe we should wait until tomorrow. I have school in the morning."

"But I want to hear the story. Please, please, please?" Mandy whined.

Good old Mandy. She turns whining into an art form.

"It's still early, Ben. Let Grandpa tell us," Dad said.

I was stuck.

"Well," Grandpa said, "the oil is indeed part of the Hanukkah story. When the Temple was destroyed, the Maccabees found a tiny bit of pure oil, enough for maybe one day, for the Temple menorah. But it lasted for eight full days. A miracle? Yes. But the greatest miracle was about faith and strength."

I turned my head so Grandpa wouldn't see me yawn.

"And teamwork," Grandpa said.

I sat up a little. "Teamwork?" What did Hanukkah have to do with teamwork? "What do you mean?"

Grandpa smiled. "Antiochus and his army destroyed the Jewish people's Holy Temple. They sacrificed unclean animals, and polluted the pure oil used to light the menorah in the Temple.

It was a disgrace. The Jews were devastated. Antiochus had a large and powerful army."

"Grandpa," Mandy interrupted, "Antiochus sounds like a big bully."

"Yes, you're right, Mandy," Grandpa said. "Antiochus was like a bully. He was a king, but he was an evil man. He wanted the Jews to give up their religious practices. For those without faith, hopelessness loomed. A small group of brave Jews, the Maccabees, ran to the surrounding hills, not in defeat but to plan their attack. They assembled an army of faithful fighters. It was not an easy or quick battle. With Judah Maccabee as their leader, they worked together in a team effort and won the battle. Their spirit, not their size, created their power and greatness."

I had never heard the story of Hanukkah told like this before. Grandpa told us about the well-armed troops of Antiochus, and the Jews with their slings, and bows and arrows. I could picture the tension on the faces of Judah

Maccabee and his army as they planned, plotted and outsmarted their enemies.

"Antiochus must have been so mad that the Jews wouldn't give in to his power," I wondered aloud.

"That's right," Grandpa said. "Antiochus was very angry that he had not been able to conquer the Jews. But he didn't give in, either. Instead he made his army even stronger. He even included trained elephants in his army."

"Elephants!" I couldn't believe it. That's the first time I ever heard that one.

Grandpa nodded with a smile, like he had seen it himself. "The Maccabees were still victorious! After many years of battling, they were finally able to return to the Temple. The Maccabees found one day's worth of pure oil to light the menorah. After sacrificing so much to protect their beliefs, you can imagine how the Jews felt when the menorah stayed lit for eight days. So you see, the miracle of the oil occurred only after the miracle of the victory over Antiochus."

I could have listened forever. I could see it all in my mind like a movie. Mandy had fallen asleep on the couch, and our empty cocoa cups sat on the table.

Dad said, "I'm glad Grandpa is here to tell you kids the story of Hanukkah, just like he told me when I was young."

Grandpa smiled. "It has been a long time. I'm just sorry Mandy missed the end!"

Mom picked up Mandy in her arms. She said, "It was a wonderful evening but it's getting late and it is a school night."

"We'll talk more tomorrow," Grandpa said.

When everyone had gone to sleep, I lay awake in bed, thoughts running through my mind. I couldn't stop thinking about Grandpa's story of the Maccabees and the small army defeating a huge enemy. I was clenching my fists; I could feel the intensity of the fight in my whole body. Just before I fell asleep, I realized I hadn't worried about Tank the whole time I was listening to Grandpa.

Ten
Teamwork

I walked into the classroom just as the bell was ringing, still thinking about Grandpa's Hanukkah story. The first part of the morning was free reading, but I left my book in Mom's van. I tried to catch Nick's eye, but he didn't look my way. Blair smiled at me again. This time I smiled back.

I went to the class bookshelf and the only thing I hadn't read before was *Science and You: Fun with Gravity*. Since I really don't care why apples fall off trees, I went back to my desk.

We were allowed to work quietly during free reading, so I decided to think about my Family Celebration Project. I looked at the holiday bulletin boards. The menorah on the Hanukkah board was colorful and festive looking, but it couldn't begin to tell the story like Grandpa did. Suddenly, it hit me: the perfect idea for my Family Celebration Project. I quickly made a list of everything I would need. I couldn't wait to get started!

When free reading was over, we moved on to board work. I volunteered to do a math problem, and actually got it right. Mr. Matthews said, "Good job, Ben. That was a tricky one!"

I forgot to bring a snack for recess, but Nick had an extra bag of chips.

I snapped the bag open.

"You still need a ride to practice today?" Nick asked me.

I wrinkled my forehead. "Well, yeah. Why wouldn't I?"

Nick shrugged. "Just wondering."

He seemed kind of quiet, and I knew why. I also knew why he'd asked me about practice. I felt like a traitor. "Sorry I didn't pass the ball to you."

"That's okay," Nick mumbled. But I knew he didn't mean it. He shook his head. "You just can't let that guy get to you."

Just then I saw Tank and his friends walking toward us. They plowed right by us and went over to some younger kids on a bench. Nick and I watched as Tank took a cookie from one of the boys and held it high above his head.

"Hey! Cut it out!" I called out before I could stop myself. It was bad enough that Tank treated me like dirt, but picking on little kids was just plain rotten. It made me think about Mandy and how mad I would be if someone bullied her.

Tank spun around like a tornado.

"Yeah, I would cut it out if I had scissors, but I don't."

His little soldiers laughed.

Tank stared at me.

My heart was thumping so loud I could hear it. I wasn't going to let him get to me. Not this time.

"I'm going to destroy you in soccer," he hissed. His hot breath blew in my face with each word.

I stood up straight. "Well, you're not just dealing with me." I pulled Nick up next to me.

Nick looked too shocked to say anything but he didn't sit down.

"Don't be so sure you're going to destroy anything," I said. Without even thinking about it, I grabbed the cookie from Tank's hand and gave it back to the little kid.

"Yeah, that's right." Nick said, his voice shaking a little.

Tank gave Nick a dirty look.

Nick backed up behind me. Actually, I think he was hiding behind me, but that's okay because at least we were still together.

Tank stood there and stared at me. I stared right back at the black center of his eyes. Grandpa wasn't there to save me, and I couldn't use Mandy as an excuse to back down. I thought Tank might punch me, but I wasn't giving in. I wondered what it would feel like if his fist went into my face. But I didn't flinch.

Finally, Tank said, "Gosh, you don't have to be so touchy, dude. I was gonna give the cookie back to the little punk." He turned and walked away with his little soldiers.

I blinked. For just a second I imagined they were wearing brass plates on their chests and holding swords, just like in Grandpa's story. Tank was as big as an elephant.

I stuck my hand in my sweatshirt pocket and pulled out a crumpled piece of tissue paper.

"What's that?" Nick asked.

I unfolded the paper dreidel that Grandpa had given me the night before and showed it to Nick. "I think it's our good luck dreidel."

Eleven
PERFECT TIMING

After school, Nick and I walked to his house so his mom could drive us to practice.

"Did you see Tank's face?" Nick was practically jumping up and down. "We were really fierce! I think he was super-scared."

Nick made me crack up. "I'm not sure about that," I said.

"We are the mighty, mighty Eagles!" He said, waving his fist in the air.

"I'm just glad we stood up to him," I said. Mostly, I was glad Nick had forgiven me for being a jerk.

There were a few kids from school walking behind us. One of them was Blair.

"Hey, Ben," she called.

I stopped. "Yeah?" What could she want from me?

"I heard what you did at recess today. That was so great. Travis is a real creep." She smiled at me again.

"Thanks," I said. "It was no big deal." My face felt hot.

"It was a big deal," Nick said. "I was there, too." He pointed to himself.

"Oh. That's nice," Blair said. "See you guys tomorrow. Bye, Ben." Then she crossed the street.

"See?" Nick said. "We're famous!"

Nick's house was all decorated for Christmas, with a huge Christmas tree in the living room. It had a gazillion ornaments on it. Some of them looked really fancy, like crystal and silver. Others were made out of stuff like cardboard and glitter. They looked like Nick and his brother had made them.

Nick's mom made us grilled cheese sandwiches for a snack. We drank root beer, which Dad never lets me have.

"Mrs. Alden, your tree is really pretty," I said.

"Thank you, Ben. How's everything with your family? Are you ready for Hanukkah? Doesn't it start tonight?" Nick's mom asked as she rinsed out the pan from the grilled cheese.

"Yeah, I guess we're ready. My dad does all the cooking. I just kind of show up," I said between bites of my sandwich.

Mrs. Alden smiled. "I ran into your mom at the grocery store yesterday, but I don't see her as much these days. She's so busy since your Grandpa moved in. Is she doing okay?"

What was she talking about? Of course my mom was doing okay. "Um, yeah. She's fine," I said, but I'm sure I looked a little confused.

She kind of ignored my answer, like she shouldn't have asked in the first place. "Boys, finish your snack and get in the car. I'll take you to practice."

Practice was really strange. There was some mix-up and the Bulldogs were assigned to our practice time, which meant we had to share the field.

When we first got there, Tank wasn't with his team. We split the field in half. After a few rounds of passing drills, I saw Tank walk in with his dad.

Nick and I looked at each other. Even though we had felt like heroes earlier, my stomach felt like it was full of bouncing balls at the sight of him. Luckily, the field is pretty big so avoiding him was no problem.

Tank's dad stayed in the stands during practice. He kept calling out things like "Hustle up, Travis!" and "Push harder, son!"

I connected all of my passes during our scrimmage, scored one goal, and had two assists.

Coach clapped his hands a few times.

"Great job, boys! Good work today!" he shouted.

After practice, I shot goals with Nick and Jason while we waited for our rides.

When the Bulldogs finished their practice, I watched Tank as he walked over to his dad. I couldn't hear anything at first, but I could see they were fighting.

Tank's dad was so big he made Tank look like a little kid. He shook his finger at Tank, right next to his face. Tank threw down his bag and started walking away. His dad shouted and Tank picked up his bag. They were walking in our direction.

Nick came up and stood next to me.

Tank and his dad walked by us. Tank was shouting but it almost sounded like crying.

"Sorry, Dad. I didn't mean it. I'm sorry. I'll try harder next time."

"Trying isn't good enough." His dad's face was all scrunched up like a monster.

After they passed us, Nick and I looked at each other.

"That was ugly," Nick said.

"Yeah, really ugly." We stood there for a minute without saying anything. Finally I said, "I hate to say it, but I think I feel a little bad for the guy."

"Me, too," Nick said.

A few minutes later Nick's mom came to pick him up. "See you tomorrow, Ben," he said.

I waved as they drove off.

Mom was late again. I was the last one to leave, but I didn't care.

"Bye, Coach," I called out.

"Good work today, Ben. Great attitude."

I knew he meant it.

Mom was alone in the van.

I threw my soccer stuff on the floor and climbed into the back seat.

"Hi, Mom."

"I got here as soon as I could. Were you waiting long?"

"Not too long," I said.

"How was soccer practice?" she asked.

"It was good today," I said.

Mom smiled. "I'm glad to hear it." Then she said, "I'm looking forward to the big game."

"Really?"

"Really," she said. "I know I've been a little distracted lately." She smiled at me but she looked tired.

I thought about what Nick's mom had asked. Maybe my mom wasn't exactly okay. Maybe my attitude wasn't helping.

"Hey Mom, I'm glad Hanukkah starts tonight," I said.

"Me too," she said. "It seems like perfect timing."

Twelve
A GREAT MIRACLE HAPPENED THERE

It was the first night of Hanukkah and I really felt like celebrating. I still got nervous when I thought of the big game, but somehow Tank didn't seem so tough anymore.

Dad was sprinkling powdered sugar on homemade donuts. Latkes and donuts? How lucky can a kid get?

"Hey, Dad!" I shouted.

"Yes, Ben?" He looked up from the donuts.

"I really like your apron!" It was the one with the dancing menorahs.

"Well, I'm happy to hear you've changed your mind. You're welcome to use it any time."

Mom laughed and shook her head.

I grabbed a donut and stuffed it in my mouth.

"You sure are hungry tonight!" Dad said.

Mandy put dreidel stickers on every flat surface she could find.

Grandpa moved the menorah to the table near the window in the front of the house. "Who knows why the menorah must be near the front window?" He clapped his hands as he asked the question.

"I know, I know!" Mandy blurted out. "It's so our friends can find us if the lights go out."

Grandpa laughed. "Well, not quite. It is to show the rest of the world how proud and strong we are during Hanukkah. It's a way of sharing our celebration with the whole world."

"Isn't that lovely!" said Mom.

The menorah stayed in the window for the rest of the holiday.

We all sang the blessings over the candles together, then the special blessing that's said on the first night only, and then we recited them in English.

Baruch ata Adonai Eloheinu melech ha-olam asher kidshanu b'mitzvotav v'tzivanu l'hadlik ner shel Hanukkah.

Baruch ata Adonai Eloheinu melech ha-olam she-asah nisim l'avoteinu, bayamim ha-heym bazman hazeh.

Baruch ata Adonai Eloheinu melech ha-olam shehecheyanu v'kiyamanu v'higianu lazman hazeh.

Blessed are You, Adonai our God, Ruler of the Universe, who has sanctified us with Your commandments, and commanded us to kindle the Hanukkah lights.

Blessed are You, Adonai our God, Ruler of the Universe, who has wrought miracles for our ancestors at this season in days of old.

75

Blessed are You, Adonai our God, Ruler of the Universe, who has kept us in life, sustaining us, and enabling us to reach this season.

Dad lit the candles. First the *shamash*, which is the main candle that lights the others, and then one candle for the first night.

Grandpa told us how each light represented the strength and faith of the Jewish people. "Proud and strong, just like Judah Maccabee." He gave Mandy and me a shiny silver dollar each. "Hanukkah gelt is traditional!"

Mom handed Mandy a silver gift bag, and Dad gave me a blue one.

Mandy opened her present, a little bear wearing a ballerina outfit. "Oh, I love it!" she squealed.

I opened my bag and peeked inside. I pulled out two pairs of blue soccer socks. Not too bad. "Thanks, Mom and Dad. I needed these."

Grandpa led us all in a game of dreidel. Mandy loved hearing Grandpa tell how the letters on the dreidel spell out A Great Miracle Happened There.

I already knew about the message on the dreidel, but this was the first time it really made sense.

We all laughed when Mom spun the dreidel gently, as if she was afraid it would break.

Dad did a little good luck dance, like he was in Las Vegas, before his turn. He held the dreidel between his palms and said, "C'mon little dreidel!"

Grandpa's face lit up as we played. At the end of the game, Mandy wound up with a pile of chocolate coins that she wrapped up in a leftover gift bag and hid in her room.

I had to admit it. The first night of Hanukkah was really fun.

Thirteen
WORKING ON THE PROJECT

Over the next couple of nights we took turns lighting the candles. When I didn't have too much homework, we played dreidel or listened to Grandpa tell a story. Grandpa gave us a silver dollar every night. Even though we knew it was coming, it still felt like a surprise. Mom and Dad gave Mandy and me pajamas. I also got a computer game, and Mandy got a doll with hair that changed color.

Hanukkah had put me in the mood to work on my Family Celebration Project. It was all planned out, but with soccer practices and Hanukkah celebrations, I hadn't had much time to work on it and figured I'd better get started.

Mom gave me an old shoebox that I painted inside and out. At the bottom of the toy chest in my closet I found a bunch of old plastic soldiers. Half of them I painted blue and the other half white. Aluminum foil was perfect for making shields and swords. I tried to make a foil menorah, but it was trickier than I thought. Paper clips and pipe cleaners didn't work, either.

In the end I drew a menorah on cardboard using a silver pen. I used an orange pen to draw the flames, and then I cut the whole thing out. I made a tiny stand for it with another small piece of cardboard. It looked pretty good!

Mandy burst into my room without knocking. "What are you doing, Ben? Are you making arts and crafts? Can I help?" She twisted a curl around her finger.

I thought for a minute. "There is something you can do. Can I borrow the elephants from your zoo kit?" I asked.

Mandy held her finger up in the air. "Toy elephants coming right up!" She bounced out of the room and came back with two elephants. She wanted to stay in my room, but I convinced her that my project was top secret, so she left me alone.

Finally, my Family Celebration Project diorama came to life. I put it in my closet because I didn't want the family to see it until my presentation.

It was my turn to light the candles that night, but I let Mandy light them since she let me use her elephants.

Fourteen
FAMILY CELEBRATION DAY

Mom offered to help me with the oral report, but I wanted to do it on my own. Mom had a great idea that I could hand out little dreidels to everyone.

There was just one thing left, but I would need Dad's expertise. When I told him my idea he said, "I'd be delighted!" He seemed to like that I asked for his help.

When the day arrived I had mixed feelings, kind of like when you're a little kid and you go to the doctor. It's yucky when he looks down your throat, but then you get a lollipop. I was a little scared about presenting my project, but once it was over, I'd be able to calm down and focus on the game, which was coming up in a few days.

The holiday show turned out to be not so bad after all. Mom, Dad, Grandpa and Mandy sat in folding chairs in the back of the auditorium next to the Aldens.

I had to sit with my class. We sat boy-girl so no one would goof off. Blair sat next to me. We were in the seats that are permanently stuck to the floor, so you can't scoot up or back. You have to be careful not to touch underneath your seat because you're likely to find someone's old gum. Yuck.

"Is that your little sister?" Blair asked after I waved to my family.

"Yup," I said. "That's Mandy, but I call her Munchkin."

"She's so cute. I like her tutu," Blair said. "I had one just like it when I was little." She smiled at me.

I got this weird tingly warm feeling like maybe I was coming down with the flu.

I hadn't seen much of Tank lately. It was like we had a secret agreement to stay out of each other's way. At the show he was sitting with his class, about three rows ahead of me. I avoided making eye contact. Besides, I had my project to worry about and my brain only had room for one potential disaster at a time.

The band played a bunch of Christmas songs and two Hanukkah songs. The chorus sang a New Year's song and one about winter weather that I'd never heard before. Nick had a short saxophone solo, and I clapped really hard for him.

As we walked back to the classroom after the show, I tried to go over my presentation in my head. Mr. Matthews had rearranged the classroom so that the parents were sitting in chairs like an audience. Most of the kids had at least one parent there. I think I had the biggest audience.

The students had to sit on the rug.

Nick went first. Even though his voice was a little shaky, Mr. Matthews kept saying what a good job he did for the first presentation. Nick talked about how his mom is Italian and she makes lasagna on Christmas Eve for their family, including all their aunts, uncles and cousins. Then he told us how every year the kids in his family make ornaments out of cardboard and stuff like pasta noodles, glitter and pipe cleaners. His project was a poster board with pictures of his family. His mom looked really proud.

Jason went next. His family celebration was the Fourth of July. They have a big party every year. One of his uncles was a juggler in the circus, and every Fourth of July they have a family juggling contest. Jason had red, white and blue tennis balls that he juggled for the class. He was really good. For his project, he gave everyone a handout that he made about the history of juggling.

Everyone's project was really cool. Mr. Matthews had a huge smile the whole time.

Finally, he called me up. Mine was the very last presentation. I felt like I was walking in slow motion as I made my way to the front of the class. I had my diorama and the bag of dreidels that Mom had given me.

First, I showed the diorama. "My family celebrates Hanukkah," I said. "Most people know that during Hanukkah, Jewish families light a menorah for eight nights, but they don't know the whole story of Hanukkah." Then I told my class about Hanukkah the way Grandpa had told me. I must have done a pretty good job because I heard someone say, "The part about the elephants is awesome."

Then I added something I hadn't practiced. "I used to think Hanukkah was only about the presents. Now I know I was wrong. My grandpa lives with us. He has taught me a lot about Hanukkah, and a lot of other things, too, that really helped with my project." I looked over at my family. They were all smiling. Grandpa gave a little wave.

Everyone clapped when I was done. I let out a huge sigh of relief. Then I passed out the dreidels, and Dad stepped out of the classroom. Mr. Matthews said since my presentation was over, I could show everyone how to play the dreidel game. He took a bag of hard candies out of his desk drawer for us to use as playing pieces.

The kids were spinning dreidels and laughing, and they kept asking me what the letters meant. Even some of the parents were playing.

Then Dad came back into the room with a tray full of hot latkes for everyone. Of course, he had put on his dancing menorah apron. Mandy beamed because she got to pass out napkins.

My whole class was celebrating Hanukkah! I couldn't believe it.

That night, after we lit the candles, I said, "Thanks for coming today, guys, and for helping with everything." It was hard to believe that in the beginning I didn't want my family there.

Before Mom or Dad could say anything, Grandpa said, "I wouldn't have missed it for the world! I learned a lot today."

"Really, Grandpa?" I said. "What did you learn?"

Grandpa rubbed his neck and said, "I learned I am too old to sit in those lousy school chairs."

I don't think I've ever seen my parents laugh so hard. I guess the Family Celebration Project was a success after all.

Fifteen
GRANDPA'S BOX

On the sixth night, Mandy finally got to open the big present. She ripped off the shiny paper so fast, it was like she was in a race. When she saw the art set complete with a little easel and twelve different colors of paint, she screeched, "I have been wanting this paint set my whole life!" She ran over to Mom and Dad and hugged them both. Then she twirled around in her tutu, holding her art set in her arms.

I opened my gift slowly, and it was worth the wait. I got a blue soccer bag with my name embroidered on the side. I guess my parents did pay attention sometimes. The bag was from the *Soccer Stuff* catalogue that I kept next to my bed. I had left the catalogue open for weeks, with the picture of the bag circled in red. "Hey, thanks, Mom and Dad. I really wanted this." I couldn't wait to show Nick.

Mom and Dad opened the photo album that Mandy and I had picked out at the community center holiday boutique. Mom especially loved that we put our school pictures in it. "Oh, this is so sweet," she said, as she turned the pages.

Then Mom handed Grandpa a present. The card had all our names on it but I didn't know what was inside. Grandpa opened the box. It was a gray cardigan sweater.

What a boring gift.

Grandpa said, "Thank you, everyone. This is perfect for chilly evenings."

Then Mandy jumped up like a nervous bunny. "Oh, I almost forgot! Grandpa! I have something special for you. I made it at school." Mandy reached into her school bag and pulled out a messily wrapped lump.

My heart sank. I thought the sweater was from all of us. Wasn't that enough? I didn't know Mandy was giving Grandpa a separate present. Why didn't anyone tell me? Outdone by my little sister. How low can a guy get?

Grandpa gently tore the paper. "Oh, sweetie, it is so beautiful." Grandpa held up a clay figure that looked like an orange blob with a tail. "I have never seen such a special kitty."

I wondered how Grandpa figured out that it was a cat.

After all the wrapping paper was cleaned up, Grandpa and I got ready for bed. I watched out of the corner of my eye as Grandpa neatly lined up his black shoes at the foot of the bed.

"Grandpa?"

"Yes, boychik?"

"I'm sorry I didn't have a present for you tonight."

"Not to worry. Like you say, it's mostly for little kids, and I am hardly that!"

"Thanks for the Hanukkah stories. You must have a lot of stories you could tell."

Grandpa nodded. "To tell you the truth, I don't have much else." He gave me a little smile that made my heart sink.

I looked around the room. My stuff was everywhere, and all Grandpa seemed to have was that old afghan blanket and perfectly lined-up black shoes. And, of course, the cardboard box under the bed.

"Grandpa?"

"Yes?"

"Um, the other day, I didn't mean to look or anything, but there was a box under your bed."

"Yes, that is my box of belongings," Grandpa said. He didn't sound annoyed that I had snooped.

The words stuck in my mouth like peanut butter, but they came out anyway. "What's in it?" I just had to know.

Grandpa got up. Was he mad after all? He bent over, pushed my soccer cleats out of the way, and pulled the box out.

"Sorry," I whispered and shoved the cleats under my bed.

"Well, I'm sure you won't be terribly interested," Grandpa said as he lifted the box onto his bed. "Rather boring. I don't have anything like computer games or even comic books, but here goes."

I jumped off my bed and sat next to Grandpa.

Grandpa's hands shook a little as he removed the tape from the box. He didn't seem to notice the tiny piece I had torn. He pulled slowly, the way you pull a bandage off of a skinned knee. When he opened the box the dusty, musty smell came back.

Grandpa leaned over and pulled out some family pictures and passed them to me, including one of Dad as a little kid painting, and his bar mitzvah picture. Dad looked goofy. It was fun to see. Grandpa also had a picture of me from when I was a little kid. It was in a red plastic frame with a magnet on the back. Somehow I was surprised that Grandpa had a picture of me. I never knew that he even thought much about me when he was living in Chicago. Since it had a magnet on it, maybe Grandpa actually had it on his refrigerator. Maybe he even looked at it every day before he moved in with us.

I picked up a picture of Grandpa and Grandma. They were all dressed up like for a wedding or something. The frame was silver but it wasn't shiny. It looked like it had been in that box for a long time.

Grandpa looked over and smiled. "Do you remember your grandma?" he asked.

"Yeah, I do. She was really nice. She gave me butterscotch candies."

Grandpa patted my knee. "Yes, boychik, she was very nice." He took off his glasses and wiped his eyes.

"I wish I had known her better," I said. I took the picture of Grandma and Grandpa and put it on my dresser. It didn't belong in a box.

Besides the pictures, there were lots of old papers, some knickknacks, a coffee mug with stains inside, and an old address book.

Grandpa rubbed his neck again and sighed. I felt bad that going through the box made him sad.

Then he reached into the bottom of the box and pulled out a faded blue ribbon with a medal hanging on it.

"What's that?" I asked.

Grandpa sat up straight and smiled. "Oh. This is a medal from my baseball team." Grandpa ran his hand over the satin.

"You played baseball?" It was hard to imagine Grandpa as a kid. "Grandpa, that's awesome! Why didn't you tell me?"

Grandpa shrugged. "You didn't ask," he said in a teasing voice.

"Were you any good?"

"Actually, I was." Grandpa sat up even taller.

"Does Dad know?"

Grandpa scratched his head. "Your dad was never really sports-minded."

"Tell me about it." I rolled my eyes.

Grandpa laughed.

I did, too. I couldn't help it.

"Your Dad, he is a good man." Grandpa said, looking over his glasses.

I nodded my head. "I know."

"Actually, boychik, you are a lot more like I was as a youngster."

Suddenly I didn't mind being called boychik; in fact I kind of liked it. Funny how things like that can change. I leaned against Grandpa's pillow as he told the story of his team.

Grandpa held the medal in his hand as if it were solid gold. "We started playing stickball in the street in our neighborhood. That's what we called it. We used a broomstick for a bat and a tennis ball for a baseball," Grandpa said as he looked at the medal. "We were pretty good, and eventually some of the boys played baseball for our high school. I was a shortstop. I was small, but I had a good arm, and a lot of speed. We had a very tough game in my last year of school. Just like you Eagles and your Bulldogs. It was an important game, and we won. I remember it like it was yesterday." As Grandpa talked he got that faraway look in his eyes like when he told Hanukkah stories.

"Is the medal from that game, Grandpa?"

"It sure is." He handed the medal to me.

It was heavier than I thought. I turned it over. It was engraved with the words, "City Champs, 1948." I touched the letters with my finger.

"Grandpa, this is so, so cool," I said as I handed the medal back to him.

Grandpa set the medal down on the bed and started digging around in the box. He pulled out another old picture. It was black and white with a grainy look.

"This is my team," he said. He leaned over my shoulder and pointed. "And there I am in the front."

I couldn't believe that the scrawny kid in the picture, the one wearing a crooked baseball cap, would grow up to be Grandpa. I turned the picture over. On the back someone had written, "Great season, Maccabee." I looked at Grandpa. "What does that mean, Grandpa?"

Grandpa peered over his glasses. "Ah," he said, smiling. That was my nickname: Maccabee."

"Like Judah Maccabee?" I asked.

Grandpa just smiled.

I didn't really need an explanation. I knew exactly what the nickname meant. My grandpa was a leader, and a team player.

"It's getting late," Grandpa said as he gently put his things back in the box. "Have a good sleep, boychik."

"You too, Grandpa."

Before I got into my bed Grandpa looked over at me. "Boychik?"

"Yeah?"

"Maybe we could go to a baseball game sometime," he said.

"Okay. That would be fun."

"Yes," said Grandpa, "That would be fun."

I climbed into bed and clicked off the light. I thought of the perfect Hanukkah gift for Grandpa.

Sixteen
LIKE A MACCABEE

The seventh night of Hanukkah came on the night before the big game. After all the candles were lit, and the gifts opened, Grandpa led the family in a few songs, including "Rock of Ages," "Hanukkah, Oh Hanukkah" and Mandy's favorite, "I Have a Little Dreidel." Mandy, of course, sang the loudest.

Mom had taken me to the mall when I told her I wanted to get Grandpa a gift. She even let me go in the store by myself to buy it so I could keep it a secret.

I reached behind the couch and pulled out a plastic shopping bag and handed it to Grandpa. "Sorry I didn't have a chance to wrap it."

Grandpa smiled and took the bag from me as though it were a priceless treasure. The bag made a crinkling sound as Grandpa pulled out a blue cap with white writing that said EAGLES SOCCER.

Grandpa put the cap on his head, a little crooked just like in his baseball picture. "Perfect size. What a wonderful gift! Thank you!"

"You're welcome, Grandpa," I said. "Hey, guys. Did you know that Grandpa is a champion baseball player?"

"Oh, right," Dad said. "It seems to me that I remember a story about that." He squinted and looked up at the ceiling as though he were trying to recall the details.

I helped Mom clean up and then got all my soccer stuff organized so I wouldn't be too rushed before the game. Everything was all set: my cleats—cleaned and polished, courtesy of

Dad—my new socks, shin guards and uniform. I put my ball in the new bag that I got for Hanukkah. I was ready.

Later that night I sat on the end of Grandpa's bed.

Grandpa looked up from his book.

I took a deep breath. "Grandpa, the other day when you said I could learn something from Judah Maccabee, you meant I shouldn't give up, didn't you? You think we can win the game."

"Well, Boychik, I don't know if you can win. But I am old enough to know that you can't win if you give up before you even start. It's true in soccer and it's true in life. You can give up, or you can be strong and do your best. And you can't do it alone. Even a leader needs his army."

I smiled. "Like a Maccabee?"

"Like a Maccabee," Grandpa said.

I gave Grandpa a kiss on the cheek, and went to bed.

Seventeen
GAME DAY

Finally, game day arrived. Mom picked me up from school to get ready for the game. Dad even came home from work early so he could be there. The air was cool and crisp, perfect weather for soccer. The field had just been mowed and the air smelled of grass. A lot of kids from school were there to watch and the stands were packed.

I could see Mom and Dad sitting with Nick's parents. Mandy sat next to Grandpa, who was wearing his Eagles Soccer cap.

I tried not to notice Tank and focused on warming up with my team. Everyone's chatting sounded like a dull buzz in my head. When the referee's whistle blew, I was ready to fight. The ball was kicked to me and I ran up the field. Tank stole the ball and kicked it all the way up to the Bulldogs' forward. The forward kicked the ball over the goalie's head, scoring the Bulldogs' first goal in the first two minutes of the game.

"That's okay, guys. We'll get it back!" I shouted. We had to keep our heads up.

After the kick-off, Jason passed the ball to me. I dribbled down the field but was cut off by Tank and lost the ball. Tank passed it to the midfielder, who took a shot and scored. Two goals for the Bulldogs; zero for the Eagles.

I got possession of the ball again, dribbled toward the goal, and kicked the ball right to Jason, but Tank stole the ball from him. I should have gone for the goal.

I could hear shouts of "Good try!" "Keep going!" "C'mon Eagles!" but my vision blurred. I had missed the opportunity.

At half-time, Coach called me to the bench.

"Sorry, Ben. I have to pull you."

No surprise. I knew I had messed up. I couldn't look at my family sitting in the stands.

Coach put Nick in for me. I gave Nick a high-five.

"Go get 'em, buddy."

"I'll try," Nick said.

The first minute Nick was in the game he was able to get possession of the ball. He dribbled down the field.

"Go Nick! Go Nick!" I shouted from the bench.

Nick dribbled past the midfielders, past Tank, and took a shot. The ball sailed. It bounced off the post and into Tank's possession. Nick tried to steal the ball and Tank pushed him. Nick fell to the ground.

I jumped up from the bench. Coach motioned for me to sit down. I wanted to run over to Nick, to make sure he was okay, but I wasn't allowed on the field.

The referee blew his whistle, and pointed to the penalty spot. Nick got up, rubbed his ankle, and signaled to Coach.

Coach turned to me. "You have to go in for Nick. He's hurt and you're the best guy to take the kick."

"Okay, Coach," I said.

Nick limped over to the bench. "Go for it, Ben!" he called out.

"You okay, Nick?" I called back as I ran onto the field.

"Yeah, I'll be fine," he yelled.

The ball was set in place. The goalie looked fierce. I glanced at the stands. Grandpa gave me a thumbs-up.

I could hear Tank's voice: "You'll never make it."

I took a deep breath. Suddenly the words "Like a Maccabee" rang in my head. I took a step back, and then ran forward, looking up slightly to eye the position of the goalie. I kicked the ball as hard as I could. I thought it was going into the goal. It hit the top of the goal, and then bounced off the goalie's hand. I groaned, but I couldn't give up now that I was back in the game.

As the ball went into play, our midfielder got the ball and passed it to me. Should I try to dribble all the way to the goal? No, Jason was wide open. I passed the ball to him. Jason carried the ball down the field and kicked it with all his might. The ball flew into the air, over the goalie's head, and into the goal. Jason scored the first goal for the Eagles. We all jumped on Jason. Nick was shouting from the bench. The score was now two to one.

The Bulldogs got possession of the ball, but missed a shot on goal.

"Lousy shot!" Tank called out to his own teammate. I could see the other defender give him a dirty look.

Now we had another chance. Once the Eagles got the ball, Jason sent the ball to me with three minutes left in the game.

I dribbled the ball and positioned myself. I slipped right by Tank and scored the tying goal just as the final whistle blew. I couldn't believe it! It felt like a dream. I'd been so afraid of facing Tank, but I did it and he couldn't stop me.

All the guys jumped on top of me, and the crowd was roaring. When I finally got up, Nick squeezed me so hard I could barely breathe. I could see my family in the stands cheering. Grandpa was waving his hat in the air.

But it wasn't over yet. There were no ties in a championship game. We had to face sudden death overtime. The first team to score would win. We held our own for the first five minutes, but then the midfielder from the Bulldogs passed the ball to their center forward, who connected his foot to the ball. As if in slow motion, the ball soared right into the top of the goal. In a split second it was over. The Bulldogs were the champs. Final score: Bulldogs three, Eagles two.

The Bulldogs jumped up and down and hugged each other. Their coach threw his hat in the air. We lined up to shake hands with them. "Good game, good game," we said to our opponents. The hardest part was watching the Bulldogs get their trophies. I thought about my shelf and how much I had wanted to make a spot for a new trophy.

I glanced over to the sidelines and saw Tank packing his bag. He had walked away without shaking hands with anyone. I saw his dad catch up with him and slap him on the back.

Tank turned around. His dad poked him in the chest and I could hear him say, "That's what I'm talking about, son. That's what I call aggressive."

Tank pulled his bag over his shoulder, but his trophy was sitting on the ground.

His dad bent over, picked up the trophy, and dusted it off with his jacket sleeve.

Somehow, I didn't feel like a loser at all.

Eighteen
THE BEST LAST NIGHT OF HANUKKAH

When Coach finished his after-game pep talk, I packed up my bag. This time, I stayed with all the other players. Win or lose, we were a team.

Dad came bounding onto the sidelines. "Good job, Ben. We thought you did great!" He hugged me.

I looked at Grandpa. "I'm sorry, Grandpa. I wanted you to see us win."

"Ben, there is nothing to apologize for. You are a true Maccabee. Your team may have lost the game, but you won the battle. You didn't lose your spirit. And you didn't get creamed." He smiled.

"You're right Grandpa we didn't get creamed. That truly is a miracle," I said, laughing.

That night, the last night of Hanukkah, was the best one I could remember since I was a little boy. Nick came over after the game so he could be with us for Hanukkah. We lit candles and Dad served latkes. They tasted better than ever. Nick ate even more than I did.

When Grandpa passed out silver dollars he gave one to Nick, too.

"I don't have one for you tonight," Grandpa said quietly.

"That's okay," I said, figuring that Grandpa must have given mine to Nick.

"I have something else for you, though." Grandpa pulled out the faded blue ribbon from his pocket.

"Grandpa, that's your medal!"

Grandpa placed the ribbon around my neck.

"It's your medal now. I want you to have it."

My heart pounded. "Grandpa, this is beyond cool!" I hugged him, and whispered in his ear, "Thanks, Maccabee."

Grandpa hugged me really tight and whispered back, "You're the Maccabee now." He patted my back.

As I looked at the lit menorah, I could feel the warmth of the holiday. Grandpa clapped to Mandy's singing, and Nick tried to learn the words, singing almost as loud as Mandy. We all played dreidel. Mandy won again, but this time she shared the chocolate coins.

As I felt Grandpa's medal around my neck, I realized that no one is too old for Hanukkah. Or miracles.

APPENDIX

THE STORY OF HANUKKAH

LET'S PLAY THE DREIDEL GAME!

DAD'S LATKE RECIPE

ABOUT THE AUTHOR

ABOUT THE ILLUSTRATOR

THE STORY OF HANUKKAH *

The story of Hanukkah happened a long, long time ago in the land of Israel. At that time, the Holy Temple in Jerusalem was the most special place for the Jewish people. Like most synagogues, the Temple contained a holy ark, a cabinet that held the Torah. Above the ark hung the Eternal Light, a unique lamp that was meant to shine all day and all night. This light did not need a light bulb or candles; it was lit using oil. Whenever it seemed as if the light was about to go out, the person in charge would pour new oil into the lamp to keep the light burning.

At the time of the Hanukkah story, a cruel king named Antiochus ruled over the Jewish people in the land of Israel. "I don't like the Jewish people," declared Antiochus. "They are so different from me. I don't celebrate Shabbat or read from the Torah, so why should they?" Antiochus ordered the Jewish people to stop being Jewish and to pray to Greek gods instead. "No more celebrating the Shabbat! No more reading the Torah!" shouted Antiochus. Antiochus sent his guards to ransack the Temple. They broke the ark, smashed the jars of oil that were used to light the Eternal Light and brought mud and garbage into the Temple.

This made the Jews very angry. One Jew named Judah Maccabee cried out, "We must stop Antiochus! We must think of ways to make him leave the land of Israel." At first, Judah's followers, called the Maccabees, were afraid. "Judah," they said, "Antiochus has so many soldiers. They carry big weapons and wear armor. He even uses elephants to fight his battles. How

118

can we Jews, who don't even have weapons, ever fight against him?" Judah replied, "If we think very hard and plan very carefully, we will be able to defeat him." It took a long time, but at last the Maccabees chased Antiochus and his men out of Israel.

As soon as Antiochus and his soldiers were gone, the Jewish people hurried to Jerusalem to clean their Temple. When they tried to light the Eternal Light, they discovered that Antiochus and his soldiers had broken all the jars of oil. They searched and searched, until at last they found one tiny jar of pure oil—enough to light the lamp for just one day. But it took eight days to make more oil! The Maccabees decided to light the lamp anyway. To their surprise, a miracle occurred and this little bit of oil lasted for eight whole days! The Jewish people could not believe their good fortune. First, their small army had chased away Antiochus' large army, and now the tiny jar of oil had lasted for eight whole days.

The Jewish people prayed and thanked God for these miracles. Every year during Hanukkah, Jews light menorahs for eight days to remember the special miracles that happened long ago.

* The transliterated word *Hanukkah* can be spelled in a number of different ways—including *Chanuakah, Channukah, Chanuka,* etc.

LET'S PLAY THE DREIDEL GAME

A dreidel is a spinning toy that has four sides. Each side has a Hebrew letter. Together, these letters represent the sentence, "A Great Miracle Happened There," referring to the miracle of Hanukkah.

To start the game, all players should have items (about 10 is fine) such as chocolate Hanukkah gelt (coins) or hard wrapped candies to be used as playing pieces. Each player puts one playing piece in the middle of the table to create a "pot." Players take turns spinning the dreidel, and follow the rules of each letter:

נ Nun – This stands for "Nothing." The player takes no action, and it is now the next player's turn.

ג Gimmel- This stands for "Get all." The player takes all of the items in the pot.

ה Hay - This stands for "Half." The player should take half of the items in the pot. If there is an odd number of items, take one more.

ש Shin – This stands for "Share." The player should put one item in the pot.

When there are no more playing pieces in the pot, each player puts a piece in the pot. The game can be played until most of the players run out of pieces. Remember, if only one player ends up with all the pieces, it is always more fun to share!

DAD'S LATKE RECIPE

Ingredients:

5 large potatoes	1/3-cup of flour
1 chopped onion	1 1/2 teaspoons salt
3 eggs, beaten	Oil for frying

Directions:

1. Grate potatoes (a food processor works best) and put in a large bowl after draining liquid.

2. Add chopped onion and salt to the potato mixture.

3. Add flour, and mix all ingredients. (Note: if mixture appears too thin, add more flour).

4. Heat approximately 3 tablespoons of oil in a large skillet or frying pan over medium heat until the oil starts to bubble.

5. Drop spoonfuls of the potato mixture into the oil (slowly - be careful not to splatter).

6. Flatten the spoonfuls gently with a metal spatula. Allow the latke to cook until lightly brown and crispy. Flip over, and repeat.

7. When all the latkes are done, place them on paper towels and dab excess oil off with another paper towel.

8. Transfer the warm latkes onto a festive tray and enjoy!

Although latkes are delicious by themselves, you may want to add some tasty toppings.

Sour Cream: Put a dollop on top of your latke and dig in! This is Ben's favorite way to eat this Hanukkah treat.

Applesauce: This is another great way to add flavor. Spoon some onto your latke and eat up! Mandy enjoys eating her latkes with applesauce.

Cinnamon Sugar: A sprinkle of cinnamon sugar will make your latke sweet and scrumptious! Top your latke with a dash and eat!

WARNING: While making latkes is fun, it is important to enjoy this activity only with adult supervision. Hot oil and stovetop flames can be dangerous.

ABOUT THE AUTHOR

Barbara Bietz has chaired and served on the Sydney Taylor Book Award Committee and maintains a blog dedicated to Jewish books for children at BarbaraBBookBlog.Blogspot.com. A freelance writer, book reviewer, and member of SCBWI, she also conducts writer's workshops for children and adults. She lives in Oak Park, California. You can learn more about her at www.BarbaraBietz.com.

ABOUT THE ILLUSTRATOR

Anita White is an award-winning artist and a native of Minnesota. She received a Bachelor of Fine Arts with honors from The Minneapolis College of Art and Design and has been an elementary school art teacher for 30 years. In 2009 she co-founded a local art crawl with painter and graphic designer Bob Schmitt, which you can read more about at http://lolaartcrawl.com/. Anita's work can be found at http://anitawhite.etsy.com. She lives in south Minneapolis with her husband and two cats, Gypsy and Ocean.